D0680604

BACK ON TRACK!

Also by Deanna Kent and Neil Hooson

Glam Prix Racers

Snazzy Cat Capers

Snazzy Cat Capers: The Fast and the Furriest

Snazzy Cat Capers: Meow or Never

For Sam, Max, Zach, Jake, Jackson, Ethan, Ella, Anna, Colton, Charlotte, Claire, Dean, Mackenzie, Parker, Tanner, Finn, Kristie, Mike, Rich, Kerri, Kim, Rob, Ophelia, Oscar, our parents and parental types, friends, librarians, and everyone who believes that sparkle and teamwork make the world more wonderful.

A Feiwel and Friends Book
An imprint of Macmillan Publishing Group, LLC
120 Broadway, New York, NY 10271
mackids.com

Our books may be purchased in bulk for promotional, educational, or business use.
Please contact your local bookseller or the Macmillan Corporate and Premium Sales Department
at (800) 221-7945 ext. 5442 or by email at MacmillanSpecialMarkets@macmillan.com.

Library of Congress Cataloging-in-Publication Data is available.

First edition, 2022
Book design by Neil Hooson and Elynn Cohen
Feiwel and Friends logo designed by Filomena Tuosto
Printed in China by 1010 Printing International Ltd., North Point, Hong Kong

ISBN 978-1-250-26540-1 (hardcover)

1 3 5 7 9 10 8 6 4 2

Fairy wings or mermaid fin,
Steal this book, your wheels will spin.

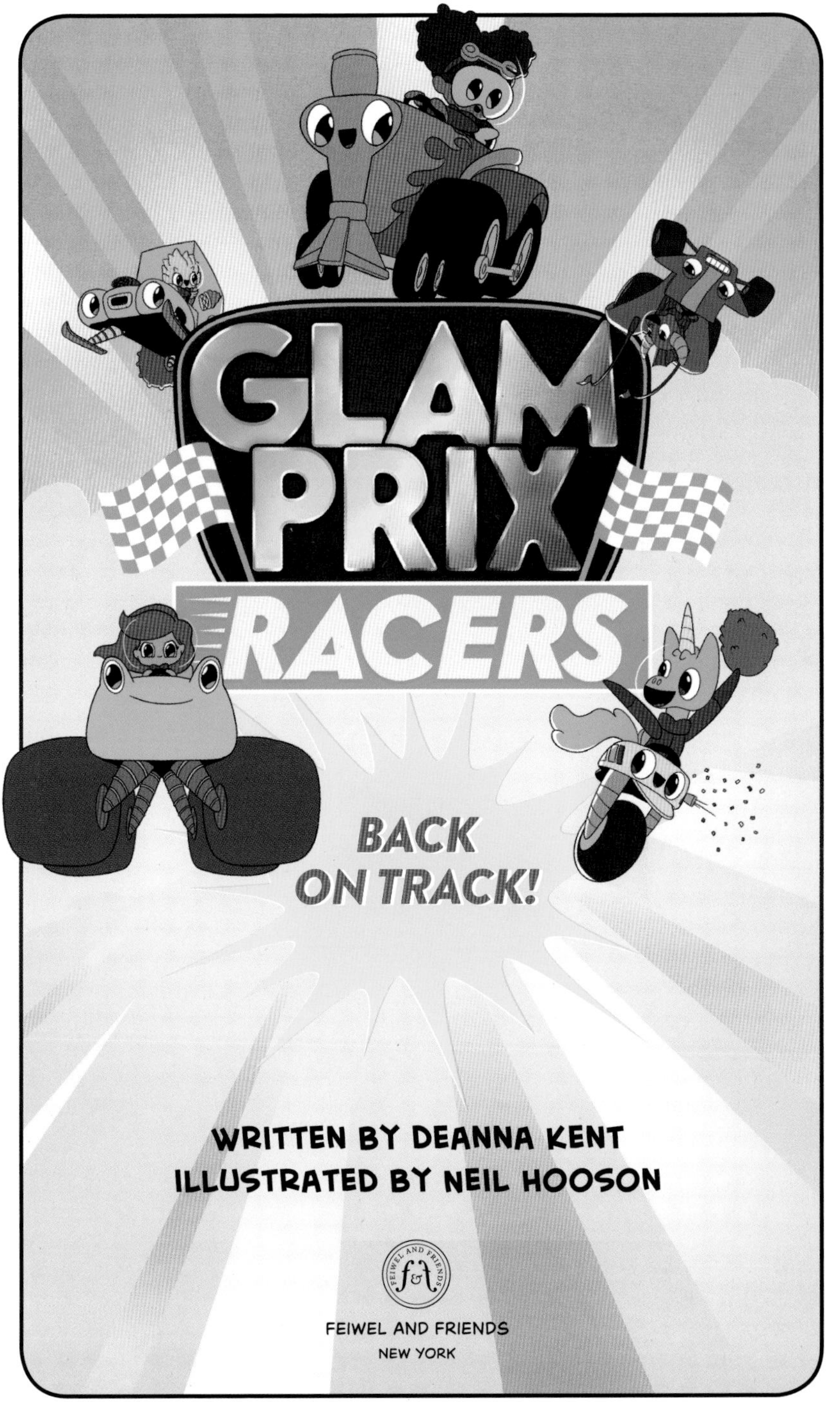

GLAM PRIX RACERS

BACK ON TRACK!

WRITTEN BY DEANNA KENT
ILLUSTRATED BY NEIL HOOSON

FEIWEL AND FRIENDS
NEW YORK

HIYA, RACE FANS! ZYAH HERE!
WELCOME TO GLITTERGEAR ISLAND, WHERE WE'RE REVVING UP FOR SEASON 1, RACE 2 OF THE GLAM PRIX!
NEW TO RACING? PRIX RHYMES WITH GLEE!
MESSY MOUNTAINS
POOF PUFFS
SPARKLECHARGE SPRINGS
COPPER CAVES
SECRET SWAMPS
DIAMOND SANDS

TWISTED TROPICS
SOFT SWIRL CITY
FANCY FOREST
ONE DAY, ZAM AND I WILL RACE IN A GLAM PRIX!
Warning: Elf confetti may alter this toy in unexpected ways.
OPAL OCEAN

MIO THE MERMAID

HOME BASE: OPAL OCEAN

TOP RACE SKILL:
SPEED

TEAM ROLE:
LEADER & MOTIVATOR

BEST TRACKS:
STRAIGHT

FLIPP THE FAIRY

HOME BASE: FANCY FOREST

TOP RACE SKILL:
ENGINEERING

TEAM ROLE:
THINKER & MAKER

BEST TRACKS:
SLIGHT SWIRLS

MOTTO: THREE CHEERS FOR EVERYTHING!
UNEE THE UNICORN
HOME BASE: POOF PUFFS
TOP RACE SKILL:
POSITIVITY
TEAM ROLE:
CHEERING & HIGH-JUMPING
BEST TRACKS:
NARROW & FAST

MOTTO: UNLEASH THE TWIRLS!
DEELUX THE DRAGON
HOME BASE: DIAMOND SANDS
TOP RACE SKILL:
TRICKS
TEAM ROLE:
FANCY MOVES
BEST TRACKS:
LOTS OF CHALLENGES

MOTTO: CREATIVITY WINS!
SOOKI THE SPRITE
HOME BASE: SOFT SWIRL CITY
TOP RACE SKILL:
CREATIVE THINKING
TEAM ROLE:
PROBLEM SOLVER
BEST TRACKS:
UNEXPECTED OBSTACLES

TO WIN THE GLAM PRIX CUP, TEAMS MUST RACE ON THREE UNIQUE TRACKS . . .
IN DIFFERENT REALMS OF GLITTERGEAR ISLAND.
RACE 1 WAS IN THE FANCY FOREST!

RACE 2 IS TOMORROW IN THE SOFT SWIRL CITY.
THE TRAFFIC IS JAMMED . . .
PEANUT BUTTERED, TOO.
WHICH TEAM WILL WIN?
CAN GLITTERGEAR ISLAND'S GLAM PRIX RACERS STAY IN FIRST PLACE?
CURRENTLY IN SECOND PLACE, WILL THE VROOMBOTS AMP UP THEIR CREATIVITY TO TAKE THE LEAD?
CAN THE CYCLOPS CAMPER CREW EAT THIS CITY UP?

GLAM PRIX
WELCOME PACK
SOFT SWIRL
CITY
WELCOME TO
GLAM PRIX
RACE 2!
WHO: YOU
WHERE: GLAM PRIX HQ
WHY: TEAM PHOTO
WHEN: CHECK IN BY 5:00 P.M. SHARP
*LATE RACERS WILL DISQUALIFY
THEIR TEAMS.
—GLAM PRIX RACE COMMITTEE

CHAPTER 1:

MESSY MOUNTAINS, MERMAIDS & MONSTER TRUCKS

PARTNER, WE ARE ***SUPERSONIC SPEED MACHINES!***

BUILT FOR MOUNTAINS!

ZOOOOOM

DID YOU CHECK THE MAP BEFORE WE STARTED CLIMBING THIS TEACUP STACK?
3:54
3:54

MAP? NOPE. I JUST SAW IT AND WANTED TO PRACTICE OUR SWIRL SPEED.

THAT'S GREAT!
BUT IS THERE A POINT WHERE THE TEACUP TRACKS RUN OUT?

OH! I DON'T—

WAAAAAAAHHHHHHH!

CRACK!

OOF!

SNORT-SNORT
SNUFF-SNUFF
HEE-HEE
HAW-HAW

THOSE TWO ARE LIKE BULLS IN A CHINA SHOP!

LET'S GO DOWN THE MOUNTAIN AND CLEAN UP BEFORE THE RACE CHECK-IN PHOTO.

HELLO? HELLOOOOO? ANYONE DOWN THERE?

WHO SAID THAT?

CLINK
CLANK

I'M TITO, TEACUP TROLL, AT YOUR SERVICE.
WELL, I **WOULD** BE AT YOUR SERVICE, BUT MY TOW TRUCK AND I ARE STUCK IN A PILE OF SOGGY TEA LEAVES. HELP US?

DON'T FRET, TITO. WE'LL RESCUE YOU!

UH, MIO?

THAT'S A MASSIVE PILE OF CUPS TO CLIMB . . .
AND MY SPARKLECHARGE IS LOW.

NO SPARKLE, NO POWER.

TITO AND HIS MOTO NEED OUR HELP.
WE'LL SOLVE THE SPARKLECHARGE PROBLEM LATER.

EMERGENCY
TEENSY-WEENSY
TROLL TEA TREATS

WHEW! WE'VE BEEN STUCK FOR DAYS.
LUCKILY, TICKTOCK AND I ALWAYS CARRY TREATS.
TITO & TICKTOCK
GET UNSTUCK!
TEACUP TROLL & TINY TOW TRUCK AT YOUR SERVICE
CALL US 24/7
LET US KNOW IF YOU'RE EVER IN A JAM.
THANKS! WE'VE REALLY GOT TO GET TO A RACE MEETING—FAST!
NICE TO MEET YOU.

THE PRE-RACE PARTY CANNON!

WE'VE GOTTA *GO*!

SORRY TO BURST YOUR BUBBLE, MIO.

WE'RE NOT GOING ANYWHERE.

WE'RE ALL OUT OF SPARKLECHARGE AND THERE ARE NO STATIONS AROUND HERE.

CHAPTER 2:

MESSY MOUNTAIN MAYHEM!

ARE WE GOING TO MISS THE OFFICIAL RACE PHOTO, GET DISQUALIFIED FROM RACE 2 . . .
. . . AND LOSE OUR CHANCE AT THE GLAM PRIX CUP?
KNOW WHAT? WITH THE HELP OF GRAVITY AND ACCELERATION, WE'RE ***SO*** GOING TO MAKE IT!

GRAVITY?
ACCELERATION?
HAVE YOU BEEN TALKING TO FLIPP?
WHEN HEAVIER OBJECTS SLIDE DOWN A SLOPE, THE DOWNWARD FORCE ACTS ON THEM TO PRODUCE ACCELERATION.

?????
IF YOU AND MUDWICK ARE GOING DOWNHILL, SINCE MUDWICK IS HEAVY . . .
YOU'LL ZOOM FAST.

JUST POINT YOUR MONSTER FACE DOWN THE MOUNTAIN!
I'LL STEER US BACK TO GLITTERGEAR HQ!

GO, GO, GO!
TWISTED TROPICS
LIBRARY OF GLITTERSHROOMS
SPLAT!
SPARKLECHARGE SPRINGS
MUSEUM OF KEYS
VROOOM

MIO! VROOMBOT GEARS AND A MISSING GENIE BOTTLE!
FANCY FOREST
GNOME GARDENS
THE VROOMBOTS HAVE BEEN PRACTICING TWIRLS . . .
. . . AND STEALING GENIES OUT OF THEIR BOTTLES.
COPPER CAVES
GLITTERGEAR'S MODERN ART GALLERY

THOSE VROOMBOTS HAVE SOME TRICKS UP THEIR METAL SLEEVES FOR THE RACE.
NO MATTER. WE'RE GONNA **WIN**.

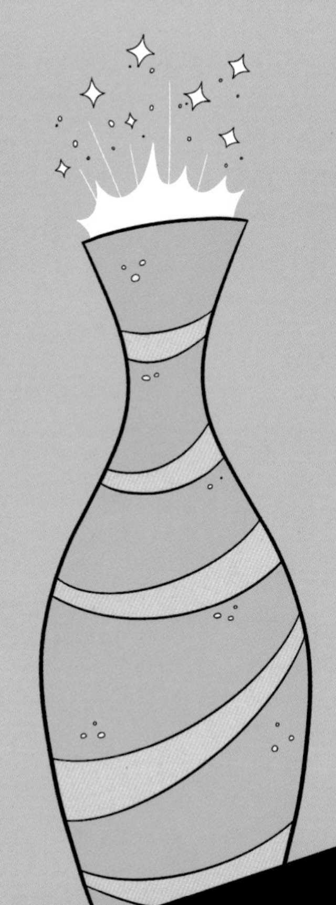

CHAPTER 3:
RACE RULES!

CLICK! FLASH!
MARVELOUS! YOU MADE IT!
DID I SEE YOU DANGLING FROM THE TEACUP TOWER A WHILE AGO?
YUP!

MIO, YOUR MOM LOOKS FIDGETY. WHAT'S THAT ***FANCY KEY*** ON HER NECKLACE?

IT'S THE GLITTER KEY. IT KEEPS ALL THE GLITTERGEAR ISLAND REALMS IN PLACE—OR MOVES THEM TO SHIFT THE TRACKS.

AHEM!

ATTENTION, PLEASE!

I'M SAD—AND A LITTLE MAD—TO TELL YOU THAT THERE HAVE BEEN REPORTS OF RACERS WHO CHEATED DURING RACE 1 IN THE FANCY FOREST.
GASP!

CHEATING? This is terrible news.

WE WANT EVERYTHING TO BE FAIR AND SQUARE ON THE RACETRACK!
THERE WILL BE EXTRA RACE OFFICIALS IN THE SOFT SWIRL CITY.

PFFSST

I JUST KNOW EACH AND EVERY ONE OF YOU—CREATURES, MOTOS, AND BOTS ALIKE—
—WILL BRING YOUR BEST TO RACE 2!

THE GLAM PRIX RACERS AND THEIR MOTOS HAVE MANY TALENTS, FROM CREATIVITY TO ENGINEERING SKILL! THIS IS THIS SEASON'S LARGEST GLAM PRIX TEAM!
MUDWICK
MIO
POWERFUL LIGHT BEAM
HARD TO MAKE SHARP TURNS
CAN FLOAT
FURIE
FLIPP
CAN TALK THROUGH SMOKESTACK
VERY STIFF, SO HARD TO TURN
ROOM FOR CARGO
CAN TOW HEAVY THINGS
DAPPER
DEELUX
FLEXIBLE FRAME FOR TRICKS
EXTRA SPRINGY
LIGHT MATERIAL, BUT CAN GET DENTED
SMOOSH
SOOKI
ICE CREAM 24/7
CAN TRAVEL EVERYWHERE
SLOW IN WATER
U-TURN
UNEE
SMALL FOR EASY TURNS
WEAK FRAME
CAN "BOING!"

This bot trio has arms and legs that get smaller and bigger. Sparklecharge lets them transform. These bots should avoid salt water, very hot weather, time warps, black opals, unicornish hens, and electric rainbow eels.
Magnetic
Removable wig
Extra brain power
V-BEST
Light and fast
V-BUFF
Loves reading
Frame can be split in half
Can carry items in torso
Heavy and strong
V-BEAT
DANCE
OFF
ON
Made to dance, but V-Best shut that off
Light and fast
So many dance moves
Can jump

CYCLOPS CAMPER

The Cyclops Camper Crew are slow, steady, single focused, and at risk for easy hypnosis. They're new to the Glittergear Island race community, but already known for their relentless snacking habits.

Camper Model 1-1

JUST AS IN RACE 1, IN TOMORROW'S RACE, YOU'LL GET POINTS FOR WINNING, AND POINTS FOR DOING SPECIAL SIDE QUESTS.
RACE MAPS WILL BE DELIVERED TONIGHT TO YOUR TEAM HQS SO YOU CAN PREPARE!
UNTIL THEN, HERE'S KIP THE KRAKEN FROM GETKRACKEN INK. WITH YOUR RULES! GOOD LUCK TO YOU ALL.
SOFT SWIRL CITY RACE POINTS
6 POINTS FOR 1ST PLACE
4 POINTS FOR 2ND PLACE
2 POINTS FOR 3RD PLACE
1 POINT FOR EACH SIDE QUEST:
SNAP A PHOTO WITH A COOKIE-DOUGH YETI.
ALL TEAM MEMBERS JUMP ACROSS LAVA CAKE LAKE.
AT LEAST ONE MEMBER OF YOUR TEAM RACES ON THE CANDY SWIRL SWITCHBACK TRACK IN LESS THAN FIVE MINUTES.
PUT YOUR TEAM FLAG UP AT THE TOP OF TRIPLEBERRY TOWER.
BRING TWENTY UNIQUE, UNUSED GLITTERGUM POWER BALLS ACROSS THE FINISH LINE.

YOUR RACE RULES: ALL GLAM PRIX RACES BEGIN AT SPARKLECHARGE SPRINGS.

AS YOU KNOW, GLAM PRIX RACE TEAM SIZES MAY BE BETWEEN THREE AND TEN CREATURES AND MOTOS . . .

BUT ALL TEAM MEMBERS MUST CROSS THE FINISH LINE TOGETHER.

THERE CAN BE NO BELLY-BUTTON LINT ON THE TRACK.

SHORTCUTS ARE ALLOWED, BUT ALL TEAM MEMBERS MUST COVER AT LEAST 85% OF THE TRACK.

THE SOFT SWIRL CITY NEEDS TO STAY COLD. NO OUTSIDE HEAT IS ALLOWED ANYWHERE.

IT'S THE LAW.

ANY TEAM MEMBER WHO DOES NOT FOLLOW THE RULES WILL BE DISQUALIFIED.

FROM THE STARTING LINE, AS AN EXTRA TEST IN CREATIVITY, YOU MUST DECIDE THE BEST WAY TO GET TO THE SOFT SWIRL CITY ENTRANCE.

WHEN YOU GET THERE, GRAB YOUR TEAM'S MYSTERY JAR! IT MAY HELP YOU ALONG THE WAY . . .

I ALMOST FORGOT TWO VERY IMPORTANT THINGS!
FIRST, WATCH FOR FROST FROG BLIZZARDS.
SECOND, BEWARE THE GUMMY MUMMY.
STAY FAR, FAR AWAY.
WHAT DO YOU KNOW ABOUT THIS GUMMY MUMMY?
IT COLLECTS RANDOM THINGS. IF YOU DON'T HAVE WHAT IT WANTS, YOU'LL BE STUCK FOR A LOOOONG TIME.
OOOOOH.

NOW GO FORTH TO YOUR TEAM HQs.

TOMORROW, ONE CREW WILL CONQUER THE TWISTED TRACKS OF THE SOFT SWIRL CITY!

We will.

And more.

CHAPTER 4:
V-SPY!

KIP FROM GETKRACKEN INK. IS BUSY DELIVERING RACE MAPS TONIGHT! IT'S AN EXCITING TIME AS ALL THREE RACE CREWS GET READY FOR TOMORROW MORNING'S START!

SO, NO HEAT AT ALL?

NO HOT PLATES?

NO HOT DOGS?

NO HOT MUSTARD?

NO HOT PEPPERS?

NO MARSHMALLOW ROASTS?!

ARE FROZEN MARSHMALLOWS A THING?

MARSHMALLOWS

EXTRA MARSHMALLOWS

BONUS MARSHMALLOWS

RARE MARSHMALLOWS

MEATLESS MARSHMALLOWS

MONOCLES

EXTRA-STRENGTH ELF CONFETTI!

MARSHMALLOW-SCENTED TOILET PAPER

MARSHMALLOW TOOTHPASTE

MARSHMALLOW-FLAVORED BEANS

GASP!

WHO EVEN ***ARE*** YOU?

No heat means no rocket booster.

I do not like that rule. I will ignore it.

We will discover the Glam Prix Racers' plans. Then we will—

Dance a disco groove like nobody's watching?

Deploy the spy drone to the Glam Prix Racers HQ.

WAH!

WAH!

WAH!

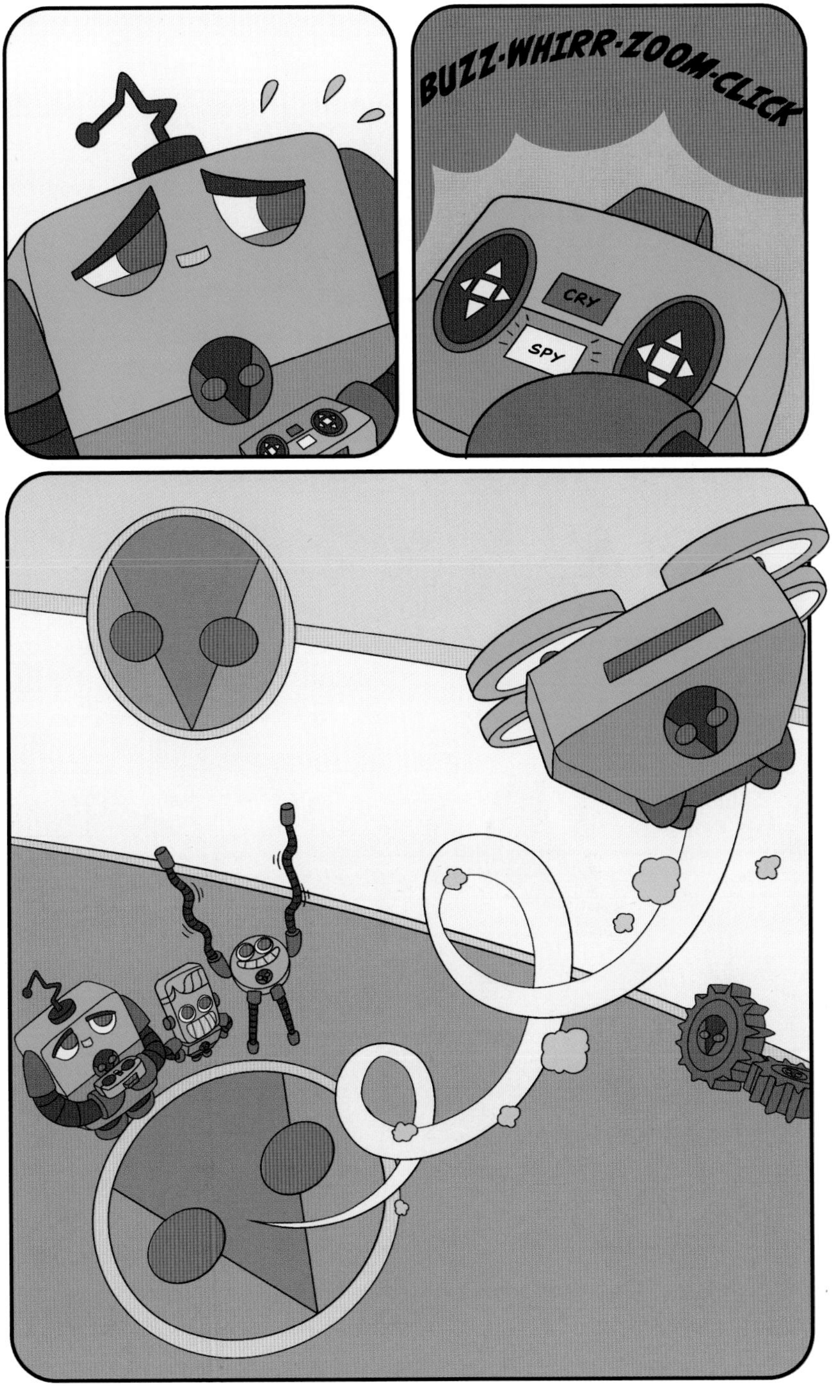

BUZZ·WHIRR·ZOOM·CLICK
CRY
SPY

VROOMBOT SPY DRONE

— LIVE FEED —

. . . STRAIGHT THROUGH THE FANCY FOREST IS THE FASTEST ROUTE!
LET'S GET EVERY SIDE-QUEST POINT WE CAN.

THIS TRACK WILL BE SLIPPERY. I'LL BRING TIRE SPIKES.

ONCE WE'RE THROUGH THE GATES, LET'S GO RIGHT TO LAVA CAKE LAKE.
WE'LL HELP EVERYONE FLIP OVER THAT CHOCOLATEY LAKE TO GET AN EASY SIDE-QUEST POINT!
I'VE NEVER, EVER SEEN A COOKIE-DOUGH YETI.
WE CAN STOP AT A SPARKLECHARGE STATION. THEN MIO AND MUDWICK CAN ZOOM THROUGH THE CANDY SWIRL SWITCHBACK TRACK FOR A BONUS POINT.
AND IF WE'RE STILL IN FRONT AT THE TRIPLEBERRY TOWER, THAT CAN BE OUR LAST SIDE QUEST!

THEN WE'LL RACE UP GUMBALL GROVE PEAK TO COLLECT TWENTY DIFFERENT GLITTERGUM POWER BALLS!
WE'LL GO AROUND GUMMY MUMMY'S SWAMP.
WE DON'T WANT TO RISK RUNNING INTO THAT STICKY MONSTER.
WE'LL BE IN FRONT!
SWIRLS AND SPEED MAKE US DIZZY, BUT WE'LL DO OUR BEST TO BE FAST.

WAS THAT A VROOMBOT DRONE?
WERE THE BOTS ***SPYING*** ON US?

And then, we will win the third race and be awarded the magical Glam Prix Cup.

Finally, we will steal all the Sparklecharge from this island.

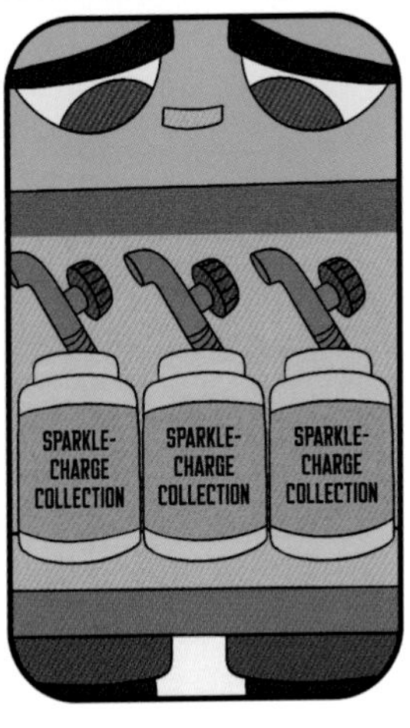

During the race, drill one hole at three of the Sparklecharge stations.
Place one collection jar in each hole.
It will fill up with Sparklecharge.
We will go back to get them after the race.
SPARKLE-CHARGE COLLECTION
SPARKLE-CHARGE COLLECTION
SPARKLE-CHARGE COLLECTION
I will be back soon. I am going to add an obstacle to the course.
DANCE
OFF
ON
Can you pick up a disco ball while you are out?
SLAM!

CHAPTER 5:
READY, SET, SWIRL!

THIS WAY TO POOF PUFFS
SHORTCUT TO SOFT SWIRL CITY
THIS WAY TO OPAL OCEAN
WE HEAR IT'S A COLD DAY IN THE SOFT SWIRL CITY. ALL THE RACERS HERE AT THE SPARKLECHARGE SPRINGS STARTING LINE LOOK ***READY TO WIN***—EXCEPT THE CYCLOPS CAMPERS. THEY LOOK READY TO EAT.
WE ALL WANT TO KNOW WHICH ROUTE EACH RACE CREW WILL CHOOSE TO GET TO THE SOFT SWIRL CITY! STAY TUNED! AT THE ENTRANCE, EACH TEAM WILL GET A ***SPECIAL JAR*** THAT COULD HELP THEM ALONG THE WAY.

DEELUX AND DAPPER! THESE UNIFORMS ARE AMAZING.

THANKS! WE DESIGNED THEM FOR THIS RACE.

TEAM, LET'S ZIP, ZOOM, AND **WIN**!

TIRE SPIKES
STICKY TIRE SPIKES
Error!
The Vroombots will win today. 
GOOD LUCK! 
Luck has nothing to do with it. Our robotics are superior.

WE'RE IN THIS TOGETHER, TEAM. EVERYTHING WE'VE EVER DONE HAS LED US TO THIS MOMENT.
WHO ARE WE?
WE'RE GLAM PRIX!
WHAT DO WE NEED?
SPARKLE AND SPEED!

TAKE YOUR MARKS!

GET SET!

GO!

ZOOOM!
VROOOOM!
BOOM!
THIS WAY TO POOF PUFFS
SHORTCUT TO SOFT SWIRL CITY

AND THEY'RE OFF! THE GLAM PRIX RACERS AND THE CYCLOPS CAMPERS ARE TAKING THE SHORTEST ROUTE TO THE SOFT SWIRL CITY THROUGH THE FANCY FOREST.
BUT THE VROOMBOTS ARE TAKING THE LONGER WAY THROUGH THE POOF PUFFS!
DO THEY KNOW SOMETHING WE DON'T KNOW? ONLY TIME AND TRACK WILL TELL!

WOOOO-WOOOO!
Is this the shortest way?
No. It is the way with no genie obstacle.
The mystery jars are here. I guess they will help with our race?
TAKE ONE
THE SOFT SWIRL CITY RACE COMMITTEE
COOKIE JAR
Take all three jars.
Should we leave two for the other race teams?
No. Take them *ALL*.

RACING FANS! THE VROOMBOTS HAVE ALREADY LANDED IN THE SOFT SWIRL CITY. THE GLAM PRIX RACERS AND CYCLOPS CAMPERS ARE THERE, TOO . . . BUT IT LOOKS LIKE THEY'RE BLOCKED.
WILL THE VROOMBOTS TAKE ADVANTAGE OF THE LEAD AND LEAVE THE OTHER TEAMS IN THE DELICIOUS CITY DUST?
WILL THE OTHER TEAMS FIND THEIR WAY INTO THE CITY BEFORE THE VROOMBOTS GET A HUGE LEAD?
SCREECH

A GENIE!

IT'S ODD TO SEE ONE HERE.

GENIES PREFER WARMER CLIMATES.

I'M PRETTY SURE WE CAN THANK THE VROOMBOTS FOR ***THIS*** SURPRISE.

OH NO! WHAT WILL WE DO?

DON'T WORRY.
WE'LL JUST ASK HER TO MOVE.

HI! I'M MIO, LEADER OF THE GLAM PRIX RACERS.
WE'RE TRYING TO WIN A RACE.
WOULD YOU PLEASE MOVE OFF THE TRACK SO WE CAN GET STARTED?
NOT A CHANCE, MERMAID. I'M BLOCKING THE TRACK BECAUSE SOMEONE MADE A WISH.
THIS IS MY LIFE'S WORK.

BLOCKING THE TRACK IS YOUR LIFE'S WORK? DO YOU THINK IT'S TIME TO FIND A NEW LIFE PATH?
DON'T JUDGE. YOU SPIN YOUR WHEELS. I GRANT WISHES. WE'RE ALL LIVING OUR BEST LIVES, PAL.
I'M NOT GOING ANYWHERE.
SHOULD WE TRY TO PERSUADE HER TO MOVE?
GENIES ARE STUBBORN. WE DON'T HAVE TIME AND SHE WON'T CHANGE HER MIND.
WE COULD MAKE A BIG JUMP AND FLY OVER HER.
NO MATTER HOW HIGH YOU JUMP, SHE'LL FIND A WAY TO BLOCK YOU.

I HAVE A SUPERSONIC IDEA.

A SUPERSONIC IDEA? EVERY TIME YOU HAVE ONE OF THOSE, SOMETHING UNEXPECTED HAPPENS . . .

EVERYONE, FOLLOW ME! CYCLOPS CAMPERS, YOU, TOO!

THANKS FOR ASKING! BUT IT'S TIME FOR OUR SNACK BREAK. YOU GO AHEAD.
WE'LL FIND OUR WAY.

CAN'T WE STAY FOR A SNACK?

CHAPTER 6:
DETOUR!

WHERE ARE WE GOING?

I KNOW A SHORTCUT THAT'LL SAVE US TIME.
PUT YOUR PEDALS TO THE METAL AND LET'S BURN SOME TRACK TO THE OPAL OCEAN.

THIS WAY TO OPAL OCEAN

HOME, SWEET HOME!

JUST THE WHALE I WAS LOOKING FOR!

WE'RE TRYING TO GET TO THE SOFT SWIRL CITY, FAST. CAN YOU BLAST US OVER THERE?

I'M PRETTY ACCURATE, BUT I DON'T HAVE ENOUGH POWER.

WHAT DO YOU NEED FOR POWER?
SPARKLECHARGE?
ELF CONFETTI?
WHATEVER IT IS, WE'LL GET IT.
MY SPOUT USES SNEEZE POWER.
I'M NOT FEELING SNEEZY TODAY.

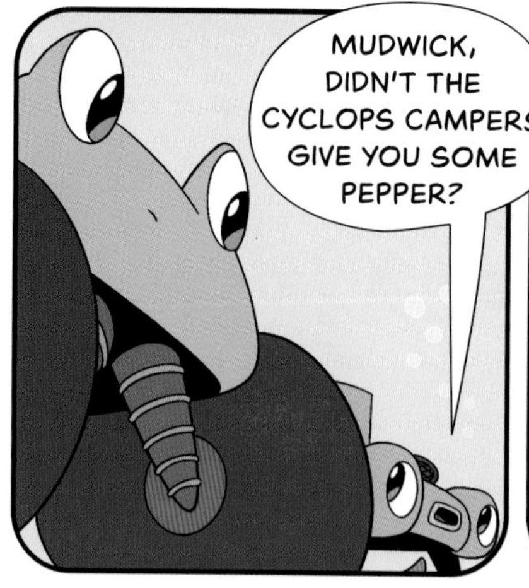
MUDWICK, DIDN'T THE CYCLOPS CAMPERS GIVE YOU SOME PEPPER?

YEAH. BUT I'M SAVING IT FOR MY CORN-ON-THE-COB SNACK.
HAND IT OVER.

OKAY! READY FOR SNEEZE ACTION?
GO FOR IT!
AH! AH! AH!
ACHOOOOOO!

TAKE
THERE ARE SUPPOSED TO BE JARS IN HERE.
TAKE ONE
THE SOFT SWIRL CITY RACE COMMITTEE
THEY'RE GONE.
I THINK I KNOW WHO TOOK THEM.
THE VROOMBOTS ARE AHEAD OF US.

DREAM TEAM! LEAVE THE DOOM!

DREAM TEAM! LET'S JUST ZOOM!

WE'RE IN IT—

—TO WIN IT!

LET'S ***GO!***

FIRST STOP, LAVA CAKE LAKE, WHERE ONE SIDE-QUEST POINT IS WAITING FOR US.

DEELUX AND DAPPER, GET READY TO SHOW OUR CREW HOW TO GET SOME AIR!

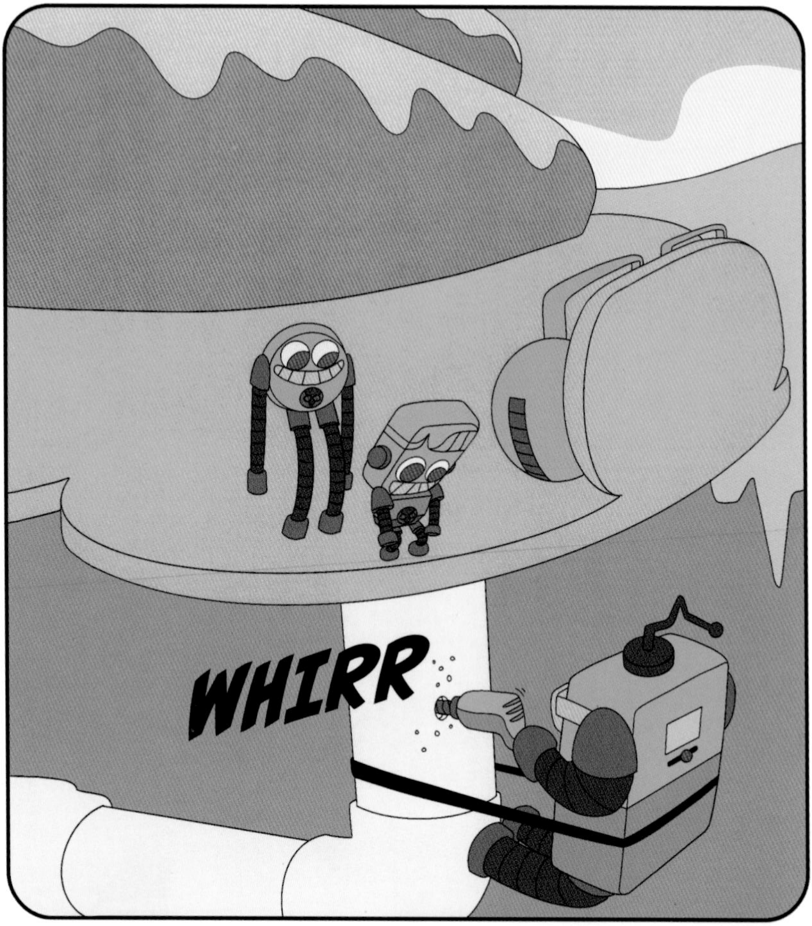

WHIRR

CLACK

CHAPTER 7: THE SOFT SWIRL CITY!

WHEEE!
IT'S THE SLICKEST TRACK WE'VE EVER BEEN ON.
LOTS OF SWIRLS AND SWITCHBACKS TO KEEP US SHARP.

AND 47%
BARFY.
ARE THOSE THE
VROOMBOTS?
WHY ARE THEY
ALREADY STOPPING FOR
SPARKLECHARGE?
LET THEM DAWDLE WHILE WE
SPEED AHEAD TO OUR FIRST
SIDE-QUEST POINT!

WELCOME TO LAVA CAKE LAKE
IT LOOKS SWEET TODAY!
IT'S GOING TO LOOK EVEN BETTER UPSIDE DOWN!

OKAY, YOU TWO. SHARE YOUR STUNT SECRETS WITH THE REST OF US.
WE'LL ALL GET SOME SPECTACULAR AIR OFF THIS RAMP.
FIRST, GO REALLY FAST.
THEN, POINT YOUR NOSE TO THE SKY.
FINALLY, LAND ON THE OTHER SIDE.
YOU MAKE IT LOOK SO EASY. OUR TRICK SKILLS AREN'T AS STRONG AS YOURS.
GIVE IT A TRY. THE WORST THAT COULD HAPPEN IS THAT YOU LAND IN THE—

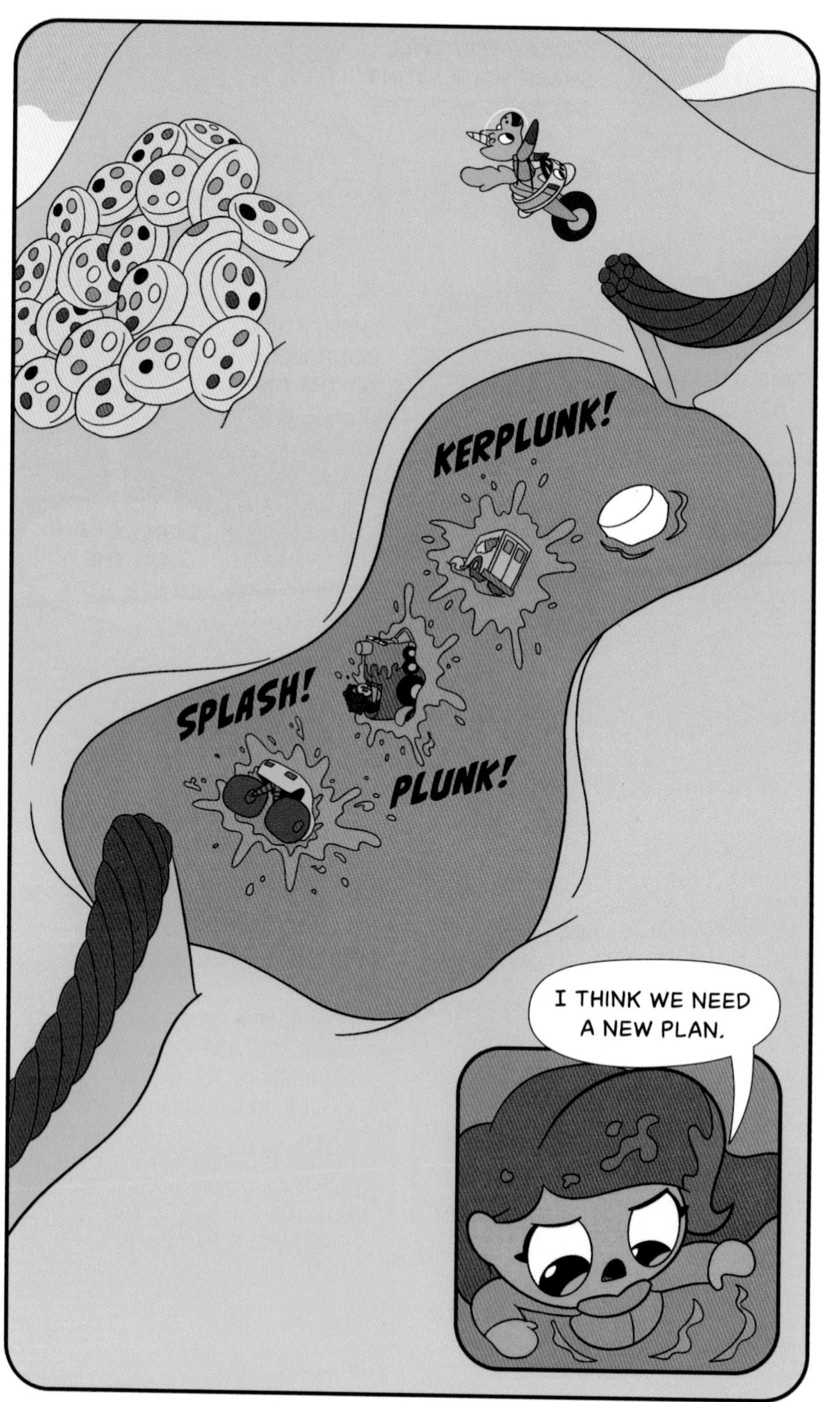
KERPLUNK!
SPLASH!
PLUNK!
I THINK WE NEED A NEW PLAN.

THERE'S A TRACK AROUND THE LAKE. WE SHOULD FORGET THIS SIDE-QUEST POINT AND RACE ON!

WAIT . . . BEFORE WE GIVE UP HERE, LET'S TRY SOME CREATIVE PROBLEM-SOLVING.

JUST TAKE A DEEP BREATH AND THROW IDEAS AT US!

NO IDEA IS BAD.

READY?
SHOUT THEM ALL OUT!

FIND A MAPLE DRAGON TO CARRY US!
MAKE A TRIPLE ROCKET BOOSTER AND BOOM-ZOOM!
BUILD A BRIDGE OUT OF RAINBOWS!
OR SPARKLES!
COOL THE LAVA AND SKATE ACROSS!
EVERYONE GROW WINGS!
EVERYONE GROW SPRINGS!

ALL OF THESE COULD WORK . . .
BUT IF WE DIVIDE AND CONQUER, WE CAN FIND MATERIALS TO BUILD A SLINGSHOT.

DEELUX AND DAPPER CAN FLING EVERYONE ACROSS. THEN THEY'LL TAKE THE JUMP.

CRUNCH

YES!

BOING

STREEETCH

HMMMM

WE'VE GOT THE BASE!

WE'VE GOT SOME STRETCHY ROPE!

WAHOO!

WE HAVE OUR FIRST RACE POINT!
SO DO THE VROOMBOTS.

NICE TEAMWORK BACK THERE. I GUESS WE'RE ALL CREATIVE IN OUR OWN WAYS.

NEXT STOP IS GUMBALL GROVE.
LET'S CLIMB TO THE PEAK AND COLLECT ***GLITTERGUM POWER BALLS***!

WE'RE GOING TO HIT MORE SLIPPERY TERRAIN UP AHEAD.

TIME FOR SPIKES!

CHAPTER 8: THE TRACK LESS TRAVELED

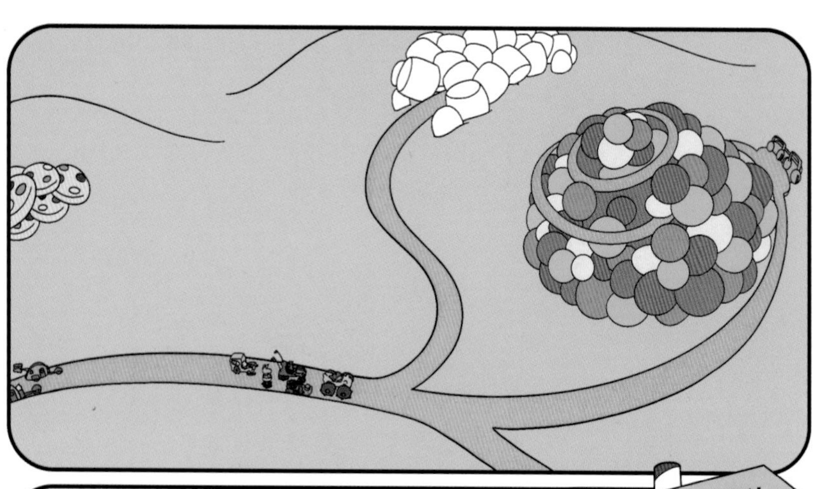

MARSHMALLOW MARSH

SPRINKLE HOT SPRINGS

WUMP WUMP

BUMP CHUMP GALUMP

CA-CHUMP!
BA-BUMP!
WA-LUMP!

FLIPP! WITH THESE
TIRE SPIKES, WERE
YOU EXPECTING FOR
US TO—

—GET 38%
SLOWER?
NO WAY.

I'LL INVESTIGATE.

THUMP-
KACHUMP-
UMP

GROAN!
HUH?
UGH!

CAN YOU GET THESE STICKY SPIKES OFF OUR TIRES AND SKIS?

NOT EASILY.
THEY'RE DESIGNED TO STAY STUCK.
WE COULD TRY TO MELT THEM OFF.

FRIENDLY REMINDER: NO HEAT ALLOWED IN THE SOFT SWIRL CITY!

WE JUST PASSED THE FORK IN THE ROAD FOR THE SPRINKLE HOT SPRINGS.
IT'S A NATURAL HEAT SOURCE.

BUT I DON'T LIKE THE AREA MUCH.
IT'S ***GUMMY MUMMY TERRITORY.***

WE'RE ALMOST AT THE HOT SPRINGS.

I'M NERVOUS. MAYBE WE SHOULD GO BACK TO THE MAIN TRACK, DRIVE REALLY FAST, AND THE STICKY SPIKES WILL EVENTUALLY WEAR OFF?!

WILL THE VROOMBOTS KEEP THEIR LEAD AND PICK UP MORE POINTS TO WIN?

CAN THE GLAM PRIX RACERS USE SPARKLE AND SPEED TO CATCH UP?

WILL THE CYCLOPS CAMPER CREW GET MESMERIZED FOREVER IN THE MARSHMALLOW MARSH?

STAY TUNED, TRACK FANS! IT'S ANYONE'S RACE!

SUCCESS! THESE SPIKES ARE MELTING.

WHILE THEY MELT, WE'LL CHECK THE TRACK AHEAD OF US.

HEY! I SPY THE VROOMBOTS! I THOUGHT THEY WERE FARTHER AHEAD.

THAT'S THEM ALL RIGHT.
THEY STOPPED AT THE SPARKLECHARGE STATION.
AGAIN? WHY? WE'RE ALL STILL FULLY CHARGED.
THIS IS THE SECOND SPARKLECHARGE STATION THEY'VE HIT.

HMMM. WHILE OUR MOTOS ARE MELTING THE SPIKES, LET'S SEE WHAT WE CAN FIND OUT.

THREE CHEERS FOR CURIOUS MINDS!

How long does this take to work?
The jars will be full tomorrow. We will come back after the race.
WHAT ARE THOSE BOTS DOING?
SCRATCH!
SCRATCH!
Onward! Go to the track.
NOT SURE, BUT I'LL BET IT'S PART OF AN EVIL PLOT.
DO NOT SCRATCH MY BACK.
I said, "Go to the track!"

BOING!

WOW! SO HERE I AM. I JUST ESCAPED THE GUMMY MUMMY'S TERRIBLE TRAP . . .

THE WHAT?
THE TRAP! ALL THE MOTOS ARE IN A CAGE!

GASP!

ZOOOOM!

GASP!

WE FOUND THE GUMMY MUMMY.

CHAPTER 9:
TUMULTUOUS TRACK!

HELLO THERE. WOULD YOU LIKE TO JOIN YOUR MOTO FRIENDS IN THE TRAP?
IT'S A COMFY SPOT.

NO, THANKS. WHAT I WOULD LIKE IS FOR YOU TO LET OUR MOTOS GO!
WE'RE IN A RACE AND WE NEED THEM.

BUT I CAUGHT THEM FAIR AND SQUARE. SO I'M KEEPING THEM.

FOREVER.
WHY DO YOU WANT TO KEEP US?!

WHY? I LOOOOOVE MOTOS.

I'VE NEVER COLLECTED SO MANY AT ONCE!

IS THERE ANYTHING ELSE YOU'RE COLLECTING RIGHT NOW, BESIDES MOTOS?

INDEED!
SUGAR BOARS, CRÈME BRÛLÉE, AND BIG BRACELETS! I'M ON A "B" STREAK THIS MONTH.

EVER HEAR OF MINIMALISM? KEEPING ONLY THE STUFF THAT SPARKS JOY?
MAYBE YOU SHOULDN'T BE HOARDING MOTOS!

YOU SAY YOU'RE COLLECTING BRACELETS?
YOU'RE IN LUCK TODAY!
?
?
?
PSSST-
PSSST-
PSSST

RUMOR HAS IT THAT THESE FOUR GIANT BRACELETS HAVE TWIRLED OVER MAGICAL LANDS!
THEY'RE GUARANTEED TO BRING YOU ***GOOD FORTUNE.***
I'LL EVEN TAKE THEM OFF THIS MOTO FOR YOU.

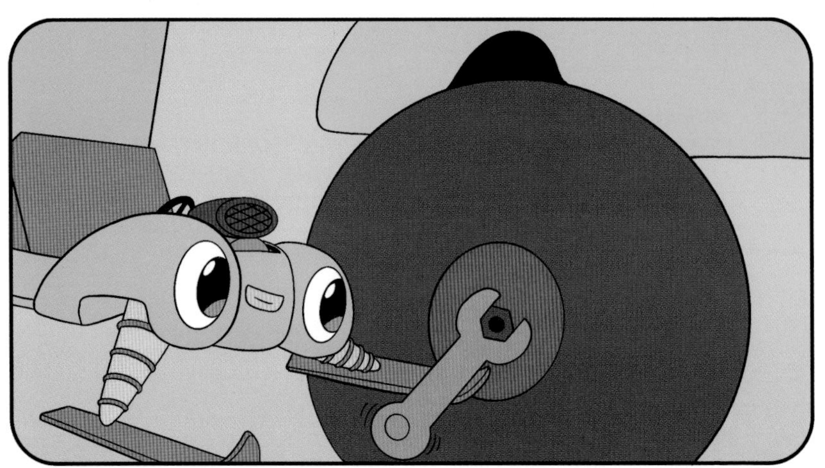

DIVINE!
THANK YOU!

WHAT JUST HAPPENED?
AM I IN THE MIDDLE OF THE WORST DREAM EVER?
WE'RE TRYING TO WIN A GLAM PRIX RACE AND I HAVE **NO WHEELS?!?**
TRUST ME. THAT WAS THE BEST AND ONLY OPTION.
TIME'S WASTING, TEAM!
FLIPP, CAN YOU FIND NEW WHEELS FOR MUDWICK?

THERE'S ALWAYS SOMETHING.
THESE WILL WORK FINE FOR A WHILE.

IT'S OKAY. MINOR SETBACK.
WE MIGHT GET MORE SPEED ON THINNER WHEELS!

SINCE WE'RE NOT LOW ON SPARKLECHARGE, LET'S RACE AHEAD!
THERE'S A LOT OF TRACK TO COVER TODAY.

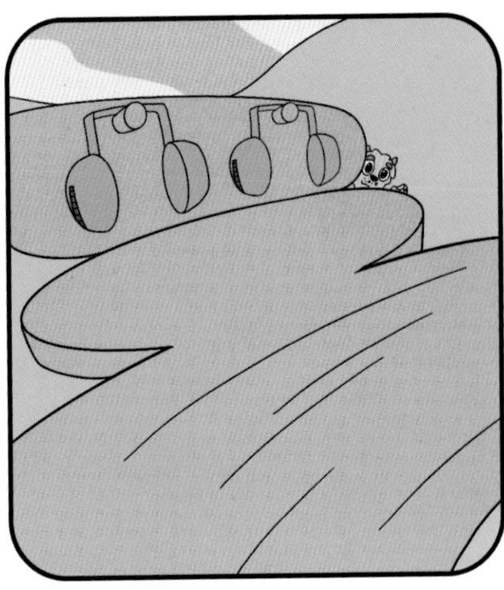

GUMBALL
GROVE
PEAK

GUMBALL GROVE PEAK, THE GLAM PRIX RACERS ARE COMING AT YOU!

IT'S GONNA BE A ***SMOOTH RACE*** FROM HERE ON OUT. RIGHT, MIO?

HA-
HA-
HA-
HA

I WOULDN'T BET MY WHEELS ON IT, PAL.

GUMBALL GROVE PEAK MARKS THE HALFWAY POINT OF RACE 2 FOR THE GLAM PRIX CUP!
WE'RE IN THE SOFT SWIRL CITY AND THE GLAM PRIX RACERS ARE CATCHING UP TO THE VROOMBOTS.
THESE AREN'T READY TO PICK.
THE RIPE GLITTERGUM POWER BALLS ARE AT THE ***TOP*** OF GUMBALL GROVE PEAK. WE NEED TO KEEP CLIMBING.

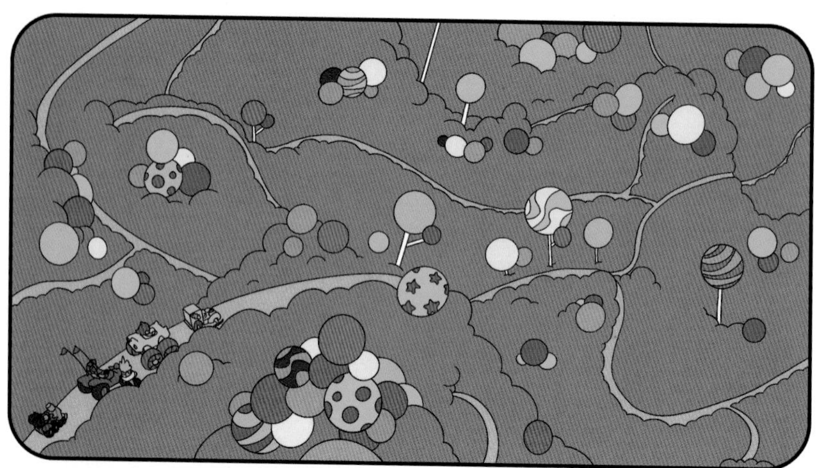

HOW'S EVERYONE DOING?

WE'RE USED TO PRETTY STRAIGHT TRACKS. JUST KEEP GOING. WE'LL CATCH UP!

WE'LL GET TO THE TOP, COLLECT OUR GLITTERGUM POWER BALLS, AND BE RIGHT BACK!

THIS IS THE MOST GORGEOUS, GLORIOUS, POWER-GUM GREENERY I'VE EVER SEEN!
WE NEED TO COLLECT TWENTY DIFFERENT UNCHEWED GLITTERGUM POWER BALLS AND BRING THEM ACROSS THE FINISH LINE.

THIS IS LIKE AN OVERGROWN MAGICAL MAZE UP HERE! THEY'RE EVERYWHERE!

IT WOULD BE A GREAT EXPERIMENT TO FIND OUT WHAT ALL THEIR POWERS ARE!

FURIE, YOU READ A LOT OF NATURE BOOKS.
WHAT DO THE DIFFERENT GLITTERGUM POWER BALLS DO?
FIELD GUIDE TO GLITTER-GUM POWER BALLS
?

I GUESS HE HASN'T READ THAT ONE YET.
I'VE HEARD THAT CHEWING RED ONES MAKES YOU EXTRA FUZZY.
GREEN ONES GIVE YOU PRICKLES.
YELLOW ONES MAKE YOU FLOAT—OR MAYBE SINK. I CAN'T REMEMBER!

LET'S COLLECT TWENTY AND SECURE OUR SIDE-QUEST POINT.

YUP. AND AFTER THAT, LET'S GET OUT OF HERE BEFORE THE GUMMY MUMMY SHOWS UP AGAIN!

IF WE NEED ANYONE TO TEST THEM, I VOLUNTEER TO TRY **ALL** THE GLITTERGUM POWER BALLS.

NOOOOO!

IN THEORY, IT WOULD BE A FUN—AND FUNNY—EXPERIMENT.
BUT IT WOULDN'T BE GOOD TO HAVE YOU CHEW ONE AND THEN SUDDENLY SHRINK INTO A MINI-MUDWICK!

OR IF YOU CHEWED A TIME-WARP GUMBALL AND JUMPED BACK IN TIME.

AS MUCH AS I'D LOVE TO TURN MUDWICK INTO A CAVEMONSTER TRUCK OR A PUPPY, WE HAVE TO GET BACK ON THE TRACK BEFORE THAT BLIZZARD HITS.

BRRRIBBIT
BRRRIBBIT
BRRRIBBIT
THAT'S A BIIIIIG FROST FROG BLIZZARD.
BRRRIBBIT
BRRRIBBIT
EVERYONE!
PICK UP A BUNCH OF DIFFERENT GUMBALLS AND THEN WE'LL BE OFF AND AWAY!

WE ARE SUPER-SPEEDY COLLECTORS!
A LITTLE INVENTION GOES A LONG WAY!
SOME CREATIVE COLLECTION HAPPENING OVER HERE!

BOING! BOING!
ROAR!
WE'LL TAKE THE HIGHEST GROUND! WOW!
WE'LL GET THE HARD-TO-REACH GLITTERGUM POWER BALLS.

WHOOOOOOSH!
WHOOOOOOOOO

WE'VE GOT THEM!
GO!

FURIE AND I CAN'T SPEED DOWN THE TWIRLS. YOU RACE AHEAD.
WE'LL CATCH UP!

WE'LL WAIT AND ALL GO DOWN TOGETHER.

EVERYONE, LOCK ARMS OR BUMPERS.

SHWOOP!
?

SWOOSH!
AAH!
THERE IS A 100% CHANCE THAT THE VROOMBOTS JUST STOLE OUR GLITTERGUM POWER BALLS WITH SOME KIND OF BOT VACUUM ATTACHMENT.
THERE IS ALSO A 100% CHANCE THAT THE VROOMBOTS JUST—
VACUUMED
EVERY
SINGLE
GLITTERGUM
IN
GUMBALL
GROVE.

MUDWICK! TEAM! WE'RE GOING TO CATCH THOSE BOTS.
WE'RE GOING TO GET OUR GLITTERGUM POWER BALLS BACK AND SPEED TO THE FINISH LINE.

CHAPTER 10:
THE HEAT IS ON

These glittergum power balls are heavy. They are slowing us down.
We are still ahead. Keep going.
Should we try to get rid of them?
Or hide them?
We will take no chances.
We must win.
Keep the glittergum power balls with you.

We will put the Glam Prix Racers in a sticky situation.
I wish we could wait here to see them get stuck in this toffee.

This toffee is frozen.
They will not get stuck in here unless we heat it up.

There is no heat allowed in the Soft Swirl City!

It is law!

I do not like that law.
Also, we are in a tunnel and zombie race officials do not have X-ray vision.

FWOOSH

This is the perfect spot for our heat blaster.

The other race crews will be trapped here.
Maybe forever.

Go!
We need the Candy Swirl Switchback Track point and the Tripleberry Tower point.
What about the cookie-dough yeti point?
I scoured the books. My conclusion: Cookie-dough yetis are most likely mythical.
Race to the last Sparklecharge station!
You will drill a hole.
You will put the final Sparklecharge collection jar in it.
We will sneak back tomorrow and collect the Sparklecharge. Once we have enough, we will take control of the island.

DARK ISN'T OUR FAVORITE. WE'RE USED TO THE BRIGHT POOF PUFFS!

I'M NOT A FAN OF THE DARK, EITHER, PALS.

BUT I'LL SHINE MY HEADLIGHTS EXTRA BRIGHT FOR YOU.

WE'LL BE LIGHTNING FAST ON THIS STRAIGHT STRETCH OF TRACK!

INDEED . . .

FULL SPEED!

SLUSHY!
STICKY!
OOF!
EWW!
GOO!
TACKY!
TOFFEE!

UGH! IF I HAD MY REGULAR WHEELS, I COULD PLOW THROUGH THIS!

BUT YOU DON'T.
SO YOU CAN'T.

SMOOSH AND I HAVE TRAVELED THIS TUNNEL THOUSANDS OF TIMES.
IT'S NEVER STICKY.

EVEN OUR HEAVY-DUTY PULLING POWER CAN'T TAKE US THROUGH THIS!

I HOPE THE RACE OFFICIALS SAW WHO DID THIS!

LOOK! IT'S A ROCKET HEAT BLASTER.
AND IT'S STILL ON!
HEAT ISN'T ALLOWED ON THE ISLAND.
GRRRR! LOOK WHO WAS HERE.

ARE WE STUCK
FOR ETERNITY?

MIO, DO YOU HAVE THAT
TEACUP TROLL'S CARD?
HE SAID TO CALL IF WE
WERE IN A JAM!
BUT THIS ISN'T
JAM—IT'S
TOFFEE!

IT SAYS TO CALL,
BUT THERE'S NO
NUMBER.
TITO & TICKTOCK
GET UNSTUCK!
TEACUP TROLL & TINY TOW
TRUCK AT YOUR SERVICE
CALL US 24/7

BUT DID
YOU ***CALL***?

HEY! TITO AND
TICKTOCK!
WE NEED
YOUR HELP!

THEY'RE IN THE MESSY MOUNTAINS.
THEY'RE NOT GOING TO HEAR—

HELLO, YOU TWO.
TITO AND TICKTOCK, TEACUP TROLL AND TOW TRUCK, AT YOUR SERVICE!

WE'RE SUPER STUCK.
THIS TOFFEE IS NO MATCH FOR OUR TOW TRUCK POWER!

WAHOO!

THANK YOU! HOW CAN WE REPAY YOU?

NO NEED! JUST RETURNING THE FAVOR FROM YESTERDAY.
YOU SHOULD REALLY SHUT THAT HEAT BLASTER OFF.
SO DANGEROUS. AND AGAINST THE LAW!

ROASTED MARSHMALLOWS!
WITH TOFFEE!

CLICK!

TALK ABOUT HAPPY CAMPERS!

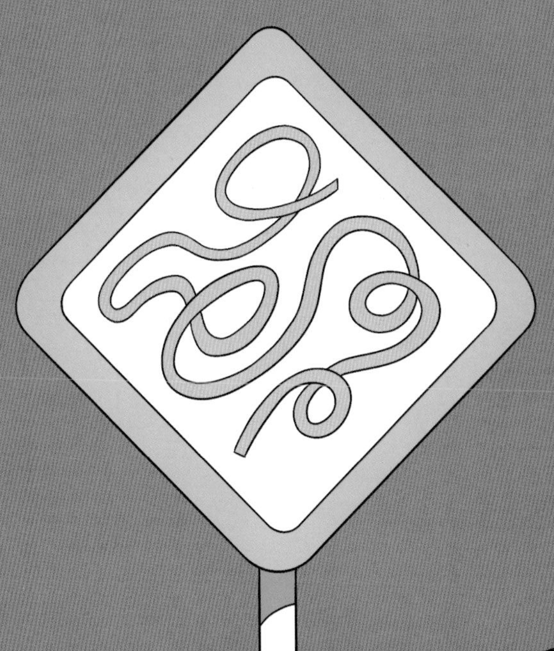

CHAPTER 11:

CITY SWIRLS

SOOKI AND SMOOSH! WHICH WAY?
WATCH FOR FALLING FONDANT
YIELD TO YETIS
SOFT SWIRL CITY CENTER
NEXT THREE EXITS
TRUST YOUR INSTINCTS THROUGH TRAFFIC.
BUT WHEN YOU SEE THE TURNOFF TO THE CANDY SWIRL SWITCHBACK TRACK, TAKE IT!

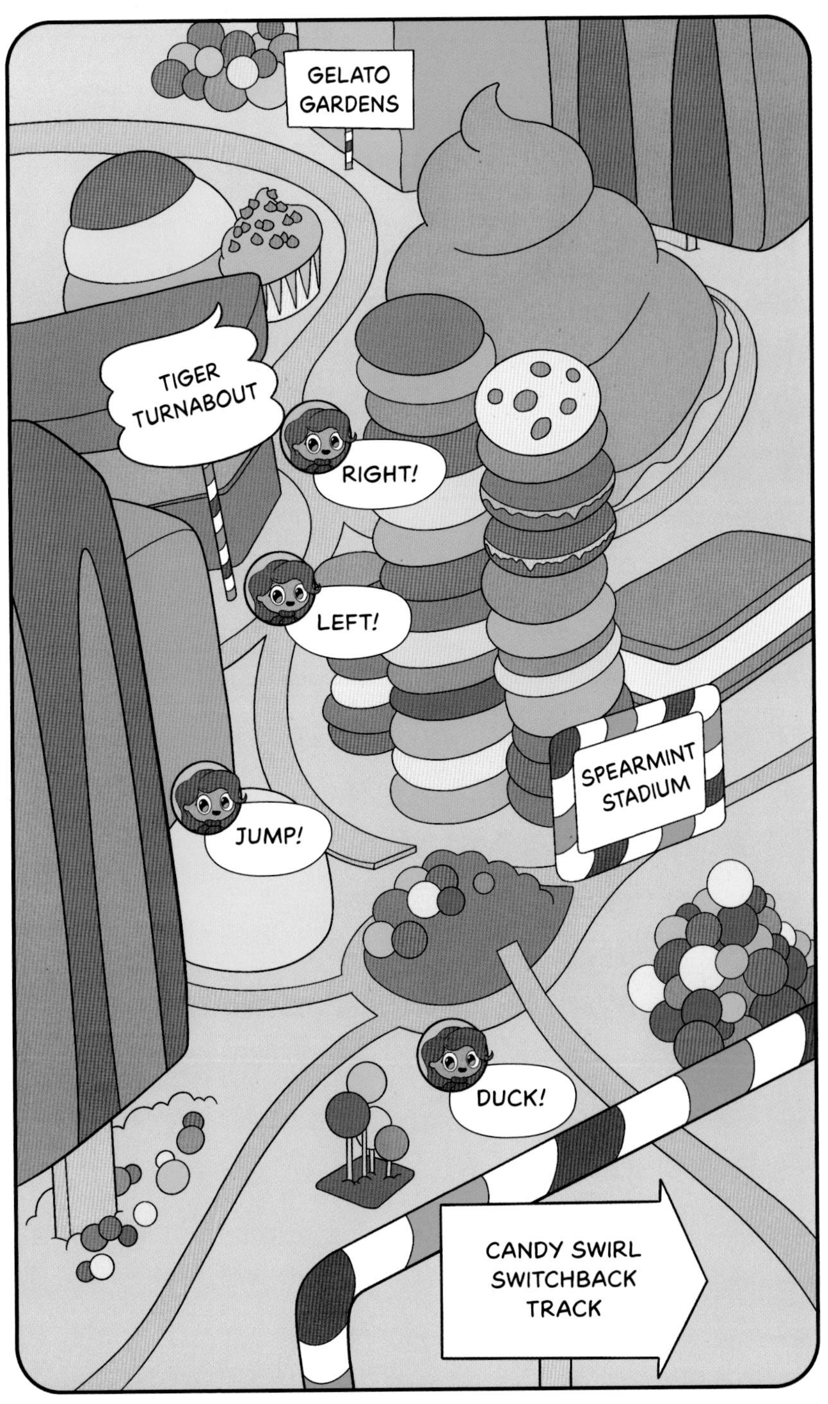
GELATO GARDENS
TIGER TURNABOUT
RIGHT!
LEFT!
SPEARMINT STADIUM
JUMP!
DUCK!
CANDY SWIRL SWITCHBACK TRACK

MIO! WE'RE STOPPING AT THIS SPARKLECHARGE STATION.

OKAY!

SPARKLECHARGE FILL-UP, THEN FULL SPEED AHEAD!

?

WHAT DO YOU THINK MADE THIS HOLE?

TOO BIG FOR A TROLL-TREASURE HOLE.

TOO SMALL FOR A DOUGHNUT-DRAGON DEN.

IT'S AN OFFICIAL GLAM PRIX RACE JAR. A COOKIE JAR . . . FILLED WITH COOKIES.
I THINK THIS IS WHAT WE WERE SUPPOSED TO GET AT THE ENTRANCE TO THE SOFT SWIRL CITY. WHY IS IT HERE?

I HAVE NO HYPOTHESIS.

LET'S PLUG THE HOLE SO NO SPARKLECHARGE PARTICLES ESCAPE.

SNIFF-SNIFF-SNIFFFFFFFF

DING!
DING!
DING!

CHARGED AND READY TO CHEER!

THROUGH THE CITY TRACKS!

YUP. FYI, IT'S RUSH HOUR!

THEN LET'S RUSH!
VROOM!

THE GLAM PRIX RACERS DON'T KNOW IT, BUT THEY'VE ALMOST CAUGHT UP WITH THE VROOMBOTS!
WE'RE HEADING TOWARD THE BUSIEST PART OF THE SOFT SWIRL CITY.
THE ACTION NEVER STOPS, FOLKS.

CANDY SWIRL SWITCH-BACK TRACK
We are ahead.
You are the fastest.
Go.

MUDWICK IS STILL GETTING USED TO HIS NEW WHEELS.
WHO CAN DO THIS TIMED TRACK THE FASTEST AND GET THIS EXTRA POINT?

THE ROAD IS NARROW.
LOTS OF SHARP TURNS.

AFTER A FEW CALCULATIONS, I THINK ***UNEE*** AND ***U-TURN*** ARE BEST FOR THIS JOB!

NO, THANKS, TEAM.

WE APPRECIATE THAT YOU BELIEVE IN OUR POWERS, BUT WE'RE THE SIDELINE CHAMPS!
YOUR IN-THE-STANDS ENERGY.

WE'VE NEVER DONE A RACE ALONE BEFORE.
WE'D RATHER CHEER.

YOU TWO CAN DO THIS. YOUR SMALL WHEEL AND SPRINGY FORCE WILL WIN THIS POINT!
YOU'RE GREAT CHEERLEADERS, BUT LET US CHEER ***YOU*** ON THIS TIME.
WHAT IF WE FAIL?

CHAPTER 12: UNICORN UNDER PRESSURE

JUST GIVE IT YOUR ALL.
IF YOU DON'T MAKE IT IN UNDER FIVE MINUTES, WE'LL KEEP GOING AND WIN THE SOFT SWIRL CITY RACE ANYWAY.

I BELIEVE IN YOU.

WE ALL BELIEVE IN YOU!

GOOD LUCK!
GO!

UNI-POWER IS OH SO . . . AWESOME-SAUCE!
SORRY, BUT NOTHING GOOD RHYMES WITH AWESOME-SAUCE.
UNI-POWER IS OH SO . . .
. . . PRETTY?
UNI-POWER . . .
. . . WINS THE SOFT SWIRL CITY!

THEY'RE NOT BAD CHEERERS!
HEY! WE'VE ALMOST CAUGHT THE BOT!
WE'RE COMING UP TO THE LAST TURN.

GET US RIGHT BESIDE THAT BOT.
DO YOU KNOW WHAT I'M THINKING?
YUP! LET'S GIVE IT ITS DANCE MOVES BACK.
DANCE
OFF
ON
DANCE **ON**, BOT!

GLAM PRIX RACERS AND VROOMBOTS!

BOTH OF YOUR TEAMS HAVE EARNED A POINT ON THE CANDY SWIRL SWITCHBACK TRACK!

CONGRATULATIONS,
UNEE AND U-TURN!

WE ALL KNEW
YOU COULD
DO IT.

YOU ARE
SPEEDY, SPRINGY
SUPERSTARS!

THROUGH THE CITY!
THE FINISH LINE IS
GETTING CLOSER.

ZOOOOOOM

AN UPDATE: RACE OFFICIALS ARE REVIEWING FOOTAGE THAT SHOWS A RACER BREAKING THE RULES.

FURTHER INVESTIGATION IS NEEDED.
STAY TUNED!

THE TEAMS ARE ALL APPROACHING THE BUSY CITY AND IT'S ANYONE'S RACE!
WHICH CREW WILL TAKE THE MOST POINTS ACROSS THE FINISH LINE?

CHAPTER 13: TRIPLEBERRY SOUR & TEAMWORK POWER!

WE HAVE A POINT FOR ALL DOING THE LAVA CAKE LAKE AND A POINT FOR THE SWITCHBACK TRACK.

WE LOST OUR GUMBALLS, AND WE HAVEN'T SEEN A COOKIE-DOUGH YETI.

GASP
WE HAVE TO TRY TO GET EVERY POINT WE CAN!
WOW, THERE GO THE BOTS—FASTER THAN EVER.
VROOM!
WE NEED OUR FLAG ON THE TOWER TO SCORE THAT POINT!
THEN WE'LL FLY TO THE FINISH!
ONWARD!
UPWARD!

ROAR!

THERE'S SOMETHING WEIRD ABOUT THE WAY THOSE VROOMBOTS ARE RACING.
IT'S HARD TO SEE THEM. FLIPP, CAN YOU PASS ME YOUR BINOCULARS?
BOING!
THEY'RE JUST A BLUR.
THEY'RE PLOWING THROUGH EVERYTHING!

HUH? MIO!
HOLD UP!

I'M SEEING
DOUBLE
TROUBLE.
IS IT POSSIBLE
THAT THE BOTS
ABOVE US AREN'T
THE REAL
VROOMBOTS?

WHY DO
YOU ASK?

BECAUSE THERE ARE BOTS ***UP THERE*** AND ALSO BOTS ***DOWN THERE*** . . .
HEADING RIGHT TOWARD THE FINISH LINE!

FLIPP! QUICK. DO YOU HAVE A ZOOM LENS?

ACME FAKE BOTS
ACME FAKE BOTS
ACME FAKE BOTS

I CAN SAY WITH 99.999% CERTAINTY THAT THE BOTS CLIMBING TRIPLEBERRY TOWER ARE **FAKE.**
THE REAL BOTS ARE CLOSING IN ON THE FINISH LINE!

SHOULD WE ABANDON THIS SIDE-QUEST POINT?

YES! DOWN THE TOWER!
WE NEED TO GET BACK ON THE MAIN TRACK TO TRY TO BEAT THE BOTS!

UGH. SORRY, TEAM.
WE CAN'T TAKE THESE TURNS ANY FASTER. THEY MAKE US DIZZY.

WHO SAID ANYTHING ABOUT TURNS? THE BOT IMPOSTORS MADE US A STRAIGHT PATH DOWN.
AND DIDN'T SOMEONE ONCE TELL US THAT GRAVITY AND ACCELERATION COME IN HANDY WHEN IT COMES TO MERMAIDS WHO LIKE SPEED?

GOGGLES ON, EVERYONE! WE'RE GOING DOWN FAST.

WHOOSH!

THERE ARE A FEW SWIRLS LEFT IN THIS SWEET CITY, BUT IT'S FULL SPEED TO THE FINISH LINE FOR THE RACERS AND THE VROOMBOTS.
THE CYCLOPS CAMPERS ARE PACKING UP THEIR CAMPSITE AT THE TOP OF TRIPLEBERRY TOWER.
AT THIS MOMENT, THE VROOMBOTS ARE AHEAD, AND THEY HAVE THE MOST POINTS!
WILL THE GLAM PRIX RACERS CATCH UP?

SLIPPERY!

YES, BUT THESE WHEELS AREN'T SO BAD!
VROOOOOOM

ANY IDEAS ABOUT HOW TO EARN OUR TEAM AN EXTRA POINT AND CROSS THE FINISH LINE FIRST?

WE'RE NOT THE MOST CREATIVE DUO HERE, BUT WHEN WE WERE ON THE SWITCHBACK TRACK, WE SAW THAT V-BUFF WAS STILL CARRYING ALL THE GLITTERGUM POWER BALLS.

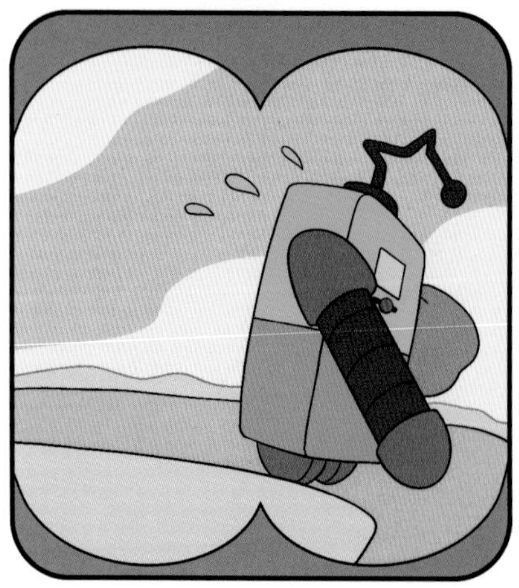

THE STOLEN GUM MAKES HIM HEAVIER. IT'S SLOWING HIM DOWN.

V-BUFF HAS A VACUUM SWITCH ON HIS BACK. I BET THERE'S A REVERSE VACUUM MODE . . .

HERE'S THE PLAN, TEAM!
WE'RE GOING TO PUSH OUR SPEED TO THE LIMIT AND CATCH UP WITH THE VROOMBOTS.

WHEN WE GET CLOSE ENOUGH TO V-BUFF, I'LL COME UP WITH A SWEET MOVE TO GET THE GLITTERGUM POWER BALLS BACK.

IT'S OUR ONLY HOPE!

CHAPTER 14:
GLITTERGUM POWER!

NOW!

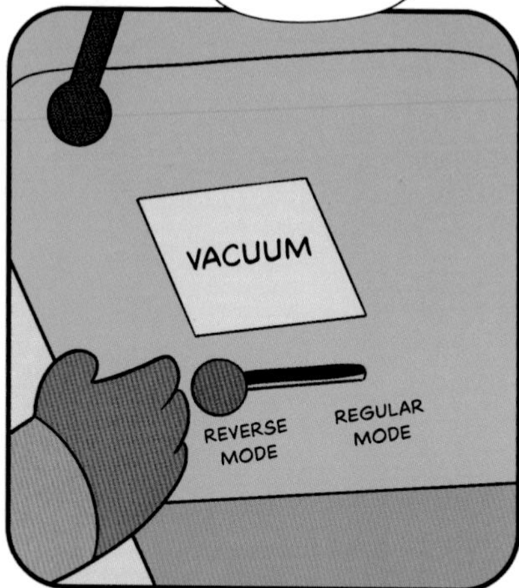
VACUUM
REVERSE MODE
REGULAR MODE

I'LL STEER! YOU JUST CATCH THEM.

HA
HA
HA

WHATEVER YOU DO, DON'T CHEW!

You may have the gumballs . . .
. . . but now we are lighter and faster.
We will cross the finish line first and win this race!
I'M OPEN TO ALL WILD IDEAS!
CHOMP-CHEW-POP-GNASH

WHAT ARE YOU DOING? STOP CHEWING!
WE DON'T KNOW WHAT COULD HAPPEN TO YOU!

I THINK THAT'S THE POINT.
I THINK MUDWICK HOPES ***SOMETHING*** INCREDIBLE WILL HAPPEN WITH ***ONE*** OF THOSE GLITTERGUM POWER BALLS TO STOP THE BOTS!

I HAVE TO SAY, I'M IMPRESSED WITH THE CREATIVE THINKING . . .

ROAR
SLURP
ZOWEE
GURGLE
PURR

WOOF!
FUZZY-WUZZY!
I CAN FLY!
WEIRD.

ROCKING!
ROAR!
HOT STUFF!
CHA-CHING!
CUTE!

CHOMP!

ALL THE GUM IS CHEWED! WE DON'T GET THE POINT!

MUDWICK'S GOT THE MATH RIGHT.
IT WAS WORTH IT TO CHEW THE GUM IF IT MEANS WE CROSS THE FINISH LINE FIRST!
REMEMBER, FIRST PLACE GETS 6 POINTS AND SECOND PLACE GETS 4 POINTS.

ZOOM
CE
ON

ALMOST THERE!

ALL THAT TRANSFORMING MADE ME TIRED.
I FEEL THE NEED FOR COOKIE SPEED!

FLIPP, THROW ME THAT JAR OF COOKIES YOU FOUND AT THE SPARKLECHARGE STATION!

WE NEVER DID
FIND OUT WHAT
THOSE COOKIES
WERE FOR.

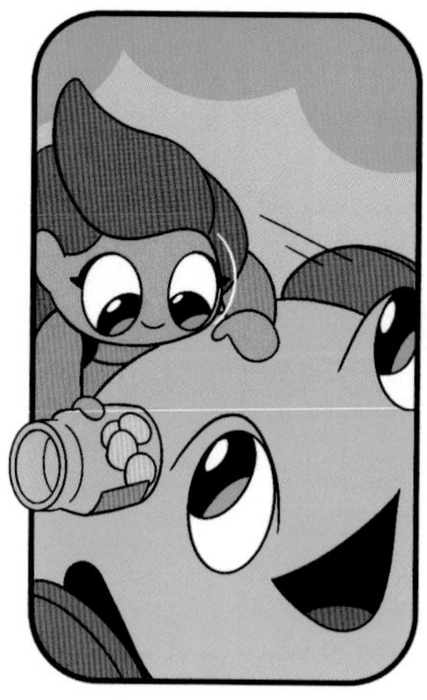

SCREEEEEEECH!

WE SMELL COOKIES!
PLEASE SHARE?

DOUGH YETIS!
PLEASE, PLEASE
MOVE.

REV-REV
Move now!

WE WERE BORN FOR COOKIES. PLEASE SHARE.
THEN WE'LL MOVE.

WAIT A MINUTE. I HAVE A QUESTION FOR YOU!

COOKIE FIRST.

YOU'RE DOUGH YETIS, RIGHT?

UH-HUH
WE ARE.

WE'VE BEEN LOOKING FOR A COOKIE-DOUGH YETI ALL OVER THE SOFT SWIRL CITY.
DO YOU KNOW WHERE THESE SUPER-SECRET CREATURES HANG OUT?

SNORT! SNORT!

HEEE-HEEE!
HA-HA!

WHAT'S SO FUNNY?

WELL, WE'RE DOUGH YETIS . . .

. . . WITH COOKIES.

SO **WE** ARE COOKIE-DOUGH YETIS!

REGULAR-DOUGH YETI.
COOKIE-DOUGH YETI.

OUR LAST POINT!
SNAP A SELFIE WITH THEM!

FLASH!
FLASH!

CHAPTER 15:

FINISH LINE!

Where is the camera?
Never mind.
We need to go! Move or we will run you DOWN.
Get down?
Get DOWN!
VROOM!

THE VROOMBOTS PULL OFF A FIRST-PLACE, DISCO-FUELED WIN!
Phew! We won.
How did that monstrosity of a truck get a cookie jar?
You were supposed to have them all!
SPARKLE-CHARGE COLLECTION
SPARKLE-CHARGE COLLECTION
SPARKLE-CHARGE COLLECTION
GASP!
Oops! I mixed up the jars.
I accidentally put the cookie jars under the Sparklecharge stations.
I guess there will be no Sparklecharge to collect.
SIZZLE!

UGH!

TEAM, DID WE JUST TAKE SECOND IN THIS RACE BECAUSE WE GAVE V-BEAT HIS DANCE POWERS BACK?!

HA! TRUE.

LISTEN, SECOND PLACE ISN'T MY FAVORITE. BUT WE TOOK ON THAT TRACK LIKE CHAMPIONS.

I'M PROUD OF US!

AND THERE'S ONE MORE GLAM PRIX RACE TO PROVE TO EVERYONE WHO'S BEST.

ATTENTION, PLEASE!
BEFORE ANY RACERS TAKE THE PODIUM, WE HAVE AN IMPORTANT ANNOUNCEMENT.

RACE OFFICIALS HAVE A PHOTO OF ONE OF THE RACERS ATTACHING A HEAT SOURCE TO THE TOFFEE TUNNEL.
HEAT IN THE SOFT SWIRL CITY IS AGAINST THE LAW. RACE RULES STATED THAT ANY RACER WHO USED A HEAT SOURCE WOULD BE ***DISQUALIFIED*** FROM THE GLAM PRIX.

V-BUFF AND V-BEAT, YOU MAY MAKE YOUR WAY UP TO THE PODIUM IN FIRST PLACE.
V-BEST, YOU HAVE BEEN DISQUALIFIED FROM THE GLAM PRIX. YOU MAY ***NOT*** PARTICIPATE IN RACE 3.

ALL QUALIFIED RACERS TO THE PODIUM!

HERE ARE THE OFFICIAL POINTS FOR TODAY'S RACERS! VROOMBOTS HAVE 8 POINTS.

FIRST PLACE: 6 PTS
LAVA CAKE LAKE JUMP: 1 PT
SWITCHBACK TRACK: 1 PT
TOTAL: 8 PTS

RACES 1 AND 2 ARE DONE WITH ONE MORE TO COME!
AND IT CAN'T GET MORE EXCITING THAN THIS!
GLAM PRIX RACERS
RACE 1 + RACE 2
= 15 POINTS
VROOMBOTS
RACE 1 + RACE 2
= 15 POINTS
CYCLOPS CAMPER CREW
RACE 1 + RACE 2
= 8 POINTS
WE HAVE A TIE TO BREAK.
RACE 3 IS GOING TO BE INTENSE!
AS ALWAYS, THERE ARE SPECIAL PRIZES FOR ALL THE RACERS.

CYCLOPS CAMPERS, YOU WIN A SOFT SWIRL FOOD TRUCK!
V-BUFF AND V-BEAT, YOU WIN DISCO GLITTERGUM POWER BALLS!
AND FOR THE GLAM PRIX RACERS, A FEW FUN ITEMS FOR THE TRACK!
CAN I PLEASE GET MY REGULAR OLD TIRES BACK?
MAGICAL WINGS, WHEELS & SKIS
YOU GOT IT.

RACING FANS! IT'S TIME TO **REV UP** FOR THE NEXT RACING ADVENTURE!
THE FINAL RACE FOR THE GLAM PRIX CUP WILL BE IN THE DIAMOND SANDS, WHERE THE TEAMS WILL NEED TO MASTER SOME MYSTERIOUS TRACKS THAT HAVE MINDS OF THEIR OWN . . .

I may be disqualified, but I am not finished here.
V-BUFF and V-BEAT, do you see the key on Queen Tallulah's neck? It is the key to all our Sparklecharge dreams.

Race 3 will be ours. We will win the cup.

WOOF!

I SAID CUP! NOT PUP!

ALL YOU NEED:
SPARKLE AND SPEED!

IT'S FUN TO
CHANGE GEARS!

RACE-FACE,
ZOOM-BOOM,
DREAM-TEAM . . .
GO!

DARE TO JUMP,
TWIRL, SPIN,
AND ***WIN!***

FUEL YOUR
CREATIVITY!

DID YOU FIND ALL TEN HIDDEN YETIS IN THE SOFT SWIRL CITY?
DOUGH YETI
WASABI YETI
CHILI YETI
SPRINKLE YETI
GRANOLA YETI
TWO-SCOOP YETI
DRAGON FRUIT YETI
HOLD-THE-ONIONS YETI
DISCO YETI
COOKIE-DOUGH YETI

ACKNOWLEDGMENTS

IN THE ACKNOWLEDGMENTS OF A BOOK, WE USUALLY SHOUT OUT ALL THE AMAZING SOULS WHO HELPED MAKE IT HAPPEN. GEMMA, ERIN, EMILY, AND ALL THE IMPRINT TEAM AND FEIWEL AND FRIENDS TEAM—WE ARE ETERNALLY GRATEFUL TO YOU. AS WE EDITED AND DID THE ROUGH DRAWINGS OF THIS BOOK, THE ENTIRE WORLD WAS IN LOCKDOWN AS A RESULT OF COVID-19. DURING THESE MONTHS, WORKERS AROUND THE GLOBE LEFT THEIR HOMES TO MAKE SURE PEOPLE HAD THINGS THEY NEEDED. IN OUR FAMILY, ONE OF OUR SONS STOCKED GROCERY STORE SHELVES AT THE KELOWNA LAKEVIEW MARKET, AND MY SISTER, A NURSE, WAS WORKING AT THE HOSPITAL. SO HERE, IN THIS WILD, BUMPY, DEVASTATING TIME, WE WANTED TO ESPECIALLY ACKNOWLEDGE ALL THE BRAVE—AND OFTEN UNSEEN AND UNDERAPPRECIATED—ESSENTIAL WORKERS EVERYWHERE WHO KEEP THE WORLD SPINNING.

ABOUT THE AUTHOR & ILLUSTRATOR

DEANNA KENT AND ***NEIL HOOSON*** HAVE WORKED ON BOOKS, BRAND AND MARKETING CAMPAIGNS, AND INTERACTIVE EXPERIENCES. DEANNA LOVES TWINKLE STRING LIGHTS, BLACK LICORICE, AND EDNA MODE, AND SHE MAY BE THE ONLY PERSON ON THE PLANET WHO SAYS "TEAMWORK MAKES THE DREAM WORK" WITHOUT A HINT OF SARCASM. NEIL IS KING OF A LES PAUL GUITAR, MAKES KILLER ENCHILADAS, AND REALLY WANTS ALIENS TO LAND IN HIS BACKYARD. BY FAR, THEIR GREATEST CREATIVE CHALLENGE IS RAISING FOUR (VERY BUSY, VERY AMAZING) BOYS. GLAM PRIX RACERS IS THEIR FIRST GRAPHIC NOVEL SERIES.